Mail Order Pearl

Widows, Brides, and Secret Babies

Cheryl Wright

MAIL ORDER PEARL
(Widows, Brides, and Secret Babies)

Copyright ©2020 by Cheryl Wright

Cover Artist: Black Widow Books

Dedication

To Margaret Tanner, my very dear friend and fellow author, for her enduring encouragement and friendship.

To Alan, my husband of over forty-six years, who has been a relentless supporter of my writing and dreams for many years.

To Virginia McKevitt, cover artist and friend, who always creates the most amazing covers for my books.

To You, my wonderful readers, who encourage me to continue writing these stories. It is such a joy knowing so many of you enjoy reading my stories as much as I love writing them for you.

Table of Contents

Dedication 3

Table of Contents 4

Chapter One... 5

Chapter Two 25

Chapter Three 41

Chapter Four... 52

Chapter Five 66

Chapter Six 78

Chapter Seven... 85

Epilogue... 93

From the Author 101

About the Author.................................. 102

Links.. 103

Chapter One

Little Rock, Montana – 1880

Pearl Hopkins stood behind the counter of *Hemsley's Mercantile*, waiting for the one remaining customer to choose his items and leave so she could close the store.

This wasn't something she normally did, but it had been quiet all afternoon, so Mr Hemsley decided to take his new wife to the local diner for their evening meal.

Making the best use of her time, she refilled the containers of rice, flour, oats and barley, and felt the customer's gaze burn a hole in her back. Pearl spun around to find the stranger staring at her.

"Do you sell flowers," he asked, glancing about.

She smiled, relieved. He was waiting for her assistance. "We certainly do. They are in the back corner." She rarely had to lock up, but it always worried her when she did. Locals she could deal with – she knew them all and trusted each one.

It was the strangers she worried about, and this one was no different.

As she pointed him toward the few flowers they had left this late in the day, he grinned. "These will do nicely, thank you," he said, bringing them to the counter.

She carefully wrapped the bouquet and handed them over. "That will be twenty-five cents," she said, holding her hand out.

He nodded, and shoved his hand into his pocket, pulling out a handful of coins. Their hands touched as he handed the money over. His were cold to her warm hands, and she shivered at the contact.

"Thank you, Sir, and have a good evening," she said, following him to the front door. The moment he was gone, she locked the door.

Pearl pottered about the store, tidying up and making sure everything was as it should be. She glanced out the window as she turned the sign to *closed* and pulled down the blinds.

He was still out there, that stranger who made her feel wary. A shiver went through her. Would he be gone when she was ready to leave? She sure hoped so.

At least she didn't have far to go home. Living on the edge of town had its benefits.

She snatched up the cash tin and locked it in the safe in the storeroom. At least she knew it would be safe tucked away in there.

She pulled her coat up around her shoulders and put on her bonnet. It was supper time and she was beginning to feel hungry. There wasn't much at home to eat, so perhaps she'd just have scrambled eggs and bacon tonight.

As she locked the back door on her way out, Pearl shivered. It wasn't cold, but she was suddenly filled with icy dread.

Was the stranger still outside the Mercantile?

She rounded the corner, and there he was, standing on the boardwalk, silhouetted by the moonlight, easily recognizable by the flowers still held in his hands.

"There you are," he said pleasantly, as though he'd been waiting.

She glanced around and saw no one. He surely couldn't be speaking to her. She pointed to her chest in silent question.

"Yes, I was talking to you Miss Mercantile." There was a touch of mirth in his voice.

"Oh!" She was surprised at his words and didn't know how else to answer. "I'm on my way home." She bit her lip. That was the worst thing she could have said. She had no idea who this stranger was, and now he might take it upon himself to follow her home.

This may not turn out well.

He stepped toward her; his arms outstretched. "These are for you."

She stared at him. What was his game? They had never met. She didn't even know his name. "I can't take those," she said, rather taken aback at his words. "I don't even know you."

His expression suddenly changed from joyful to stony-faced. "Of course. I apologize profusely. Allow me to introduce myself – Joseph Canning at your service." He did a mock bow. "Now it is your turn."

She shuddered. Something didn't sit right, she felt cornered. "Pearl Hopkins," she said quietly, then began to back off.

"Please don't go," he said gently. "I mean no harm. When I saw you in the Mercantile, I had this feeling." He handed her the flowers. "I bought these especially for you."

"Thank you, but what do you mean you had a feeling?" His words had piqued her curiosity but also had her concerned.

He grinned. "Your flaming red hair drew me to you at first, your beauty and your gentle voice cinched the deal." He grinned again.

She didn't know what to think.

"Would you accompany me to supper, Miss Hopkins," he asked, and Pearl was taken aback once more.

"Well, I am hungry," she said. And it might stop him from following her home, so what harm would it do?

He watched her closely. "So that's a yes?"

She nodded and he hooked his arm through hers. That feeling of dread filled her once more, but Pearl felt helpless to stop it.

Why she ever doubted Joseph Canning, Pearl would never know. He was a total gentleman throughout supper and the rest of the evening. In fact, he was charming. She'd never met anyone like him before.

She glanced at him over her mug of coffee. He could do with a shave, and perhaps a haircut, but he was well-dressed and even funny at times.

"Where did you say you were from, Mr Canning?"

He stared momentarily. "I didn't." For a minute she worried she's said the wrong thing. "I'm new to these parts," he finally said. "I bought a ranch about half an hour out of Little Rock."

"Oh, the old Wilson ranch! I haven't been up there for years. It was well before old Mr Wilson died." She took another gulp of her coffee. "I heard it was a right mess."

"I'm still cleaning it up," he said. "At least the livestock are all in good condition."

She delved into the deepest recesses of her mind. Did Mr Wilson have livestock? She couldn't remember. Even if he did, surely they would have been sold long before this. The old man had died years ago – who has been looking after his herd in the meantime?

These questions troubled her, and she took another mouthful of coffee then decided it was time to retreat. The most troubling question of all was how she would get home without Mr Canning discovering where she lived?

She glanced out the window – it was pitch black now, and she would have to get home guided only by the moonlight.

"Don't worry," he said gently, reaching for her hand. "I'll walk you home. No gentleman would allow a young woman to walk home alone in this darkness.

She smiled at him feeling far from happy. This was of her own doing, but she'd been pushed into a corner outside the store and couldn't refuse him.

If he'd been a stranger drifting through town, she would have felt more comfortable because she'd never see him again. But he wasn't a drifter, he was staying right where he was.

The weirdest thing was he'd done nothing to make her feel like this – it was simply a sixth sense. An intuition, if you will.

They finished their drinks and Mr Canning paid the bill. "Thank you for a lovely evening, Mr Canning," she said as they left the diner. "I'll be fine – I've walked home in the dark many times before."

For a fleeting moment he looked annoyed. "Are you trying to get rid of me, Miss Hopkins? I told you, I'm a gentleman, and would never harm you." He flashed a smile at her, and she felt far better.

"Of course you are," she said, then hooked her arm through his. They were soon on their way.

The next weeks passed in a blur. Pearl found herself being courted by the delightful Mr Canning. Each time he came calling his appearance was immaculate. He not once had even the slightest hint of needing a shave and his hair was cut to perfection.

Despite being a rancher, he always wore his best suit when he visited her and finished it off with a tie and polished shoes.

He hired a buggy from the livery one Saturday and they went out into the forest. There he took her for a stroll, and they picnicked on the grass, on a blanket he'd brought along with him.

Another day they went to the bakery for coffee and cake. They had supper at the only diner in town at least two more times. Miss Nancy flashed her a look that said she liked Pearl's suitor.

She had to admit he was growing on her and was a perfect gentleman. He'd not even tried to kiss her once.

There was a time that every day rolled into the next with the exception of her part-time job at *Hemsley's Mercantile.* That was until Joseph Canning came along. Now her life seemed to have more meaning.

Pearl sat at her dressing table brushing her hair before bed. Fifty strokes every night before retiring. That was what her mother taught her, and that's what she continued to do well after Mother had died.

Joseph was picking her up in the morning at ten and told her to wear her best clothes. He had a surprise for her but wouldn't say more.

She finished brushing her hair and flicked through her limited wardrobe of clothes. She eyed the pretty pink dress she'd bought a little over a year ago to wear to dances, but Little Rock hadn't held a dance for a year, so it had been barely worn.

The thought entered her mind he was taking her dancing, but at ten in the morning? That was highly unlikely.

Pearl found her white boots to wear with the dress and put them both aside, then lay down on the bed and rested her head on the pillow.

Pulling the covers up to her chin, she drifted off to sleep with visions of dancing close to Joseph Canning running through her mind.

Pearl was frightened awake by pounding on the front door. She pulled her robe around her and stumbled to the door in a half awake/half asleep stupor.

What could be so important?

She gingerly opened the door, glancing around it. Looking more handsome than she'd ever seen him was Joseph.

He grinned down at her, then reached out and brushed her disheveled hair out of her face. "Good morning, my darling," he said in the sweetest voice she'd ever heard. "Did I wake you?"

She nodded but didn't get a chance to answer. He pulled her close and kissed her right on the lips!

"You do look delicious, I must say," he said, winking at her.

Pearl took a step back. What had gotten into him? "Did I sleep in? What time is it?" she asked, her voice slightly husky. She needed a drink – her mouth was dry.

"Half eight," he said, checking his pocket-watch.

"Really? You said you'd pick me up at ten." What was he thinking? "You'll have to leave so I can get ready," she said, pushing the door closed, but he shoved his foot there stopping her. She stared at him suspiciously. "You can't come in," she said firmly. "That would not be proper."

He left his foot where it was. "What am I supposed to do in the meantime?" he asked in a little boy whiney voice.

She stared at him. Then he suddenly grinned. "I'm fooling around. I'll come back in thirty minutes, maybe an hour? I wanted to ensure you'd be ready on time."

She had never taken over an hour to get ready and wasn't about to start now. She suddenly felt annoyed.

He leaned forward and gently kissed her cheek. "Don't be late – I have big plans for today," he said, cupping her cheek in his hand. He turned and walked back toward town.

Pearl closed and locked the door, then began to get ready for the big surprise. Knowing Joseph, it would be very special. Likely a day to remember.

~*~

Pearl found herself standing outside the preacher's house.

She'd grown up with Preacher Jones. He'd married her parents, and just about everyone else in Little Rock. She attended church every Sunday and knew him better than most other people in town.

She stared up at Joseph. "What's going on?" She was more than a little confused.

He grinned. "You haven't worked it out yet? We're getting married."

She gasped. "What? No!"

"You don't love me," he asked half-joking.

She wasn't sure how to answer. They hadn't known each other *that* long. "I, uh,"

Heavy footsteps headed toward the door. He grabbed Pearl by the arm and pulled her close beside him. "Do you feel that?" he asked, guiding her hand to the pocket of his suit. "If you want the preacher to live, you will marry me without protest."

Her heart thudded. This wasn't the Joseph she knew. "I, I don't understand." She didn't recognize her own voice, it trembled so much.

The door to the manse opened. "Ah Miss Hopkins. Good morning." He smiled as though he was truly happy to see her. "And who is this young gent?"

Joseph squeezed her hand tightly. "Good morning, Preacher Jones," he said pleasantly. "I am Joseph Canning. Pearl and I want to get married."

The preacher frowned. "Is that right, Miss Hopkins?"

Joseph squeezed her hand in warning, and she nodded. She couldn't bear to see anything happen to this dear man or his lovely wife.

"Absolutely," she said, putting on the best smile she could. "The sooner the better."

"Well then, come on in. I'll round up Mrs Jones and get Mrs Grayson too. She's next door cleaning the church." He winked at her. "We need our two witnesses to go ahead."

"I didn't give that a thought, Preacher," Joseph told him, sounding completely innocent.

He indicated they sit down on the sofa in the sitting room, then left to get their witnesses. The moment he was gone, Pearl rounded on him. "What's this about, Joseph? Is it another one of your jokes?"

He reached for her hand and slipped it into his suit pocket. The cold metallic object startled her, and she quickly pulled her hand back. "Is that…?"

"You know exactly what it is," he snarled, and she couldn't believe this was the same man who'd courted her over the past weeks.

He stood as two women entered the room. "I can't thank you enough," he said, behaving as though nothing was amiss.

For a moment Pearl thought she must have dreamed it all. The moment he pulled her to her feet and pushed her hand against his pocket as reassurance, she knew it was a living nightmare.

The next ten minutes passed in a blur. She couldn't recall a word the preacher had said. "I now pronounce you man and wife," he said then turned to Joseph. "You may now kiss your bride."

She swallowed. Was this really happening? It would be such a blessed day any other time, but this? Her marriage was not meant to happen this way.

Joseph cupped her cheeks and kissed her on the lips. She was beginning to fall in love with him, and now this. She'd dreamed of this moment since she was a little girl playing dress-ups. Never in her wildest dreams did she believe she'd be forced into marriage.

The preacher stepped forward as they separated and hugged her. "I am so very happy for you, Miss Hopkins. Oh, Mrs Canning!" he said, winking. "I'm sure you'll both enjoy a lifetime of love."

"Thank you, preacher," Joseph said, reaching into his pocket and pulling out a wad of notes. He handed the preacher one hundred dollars, and the preacher's eyes opened wide. He looked as shocked as Pearl felt.

"No, my boy. I couldn't possibly take that."

Joseph leaned in. "Of course you can," he said quietly. "Take some of it for your time. The rest... I'm sure you can find a worthy cause within the church. Food baskets, clothing for poorer families? Whatever you please."

Preacher Jones put his hand to Joseph's shoulder. "Thank you, my boy. You are a man among men."

Pearl did her best not to scoff. If only the preacher knew the truth. She wanted to tell him, but dare not risk his life, or that of their witnesses.

"Thank you again," Joseph said. "We have a long ride home, so we must be off now."

"You're not celebrating in town?" Mrs Jones asked.

Pearl swallowed hard. She watched the tick on Joseph's forehead and hoped he calmed down. She'd noticed it the moment she'd refused to cooperate with him. Strangely enough, she'd never noticed it before today.

"I have a small celebration arranged at home," he said, then headed toward the front door. "Thank you all again. We both appreciate it, don't we darling?" He almost snickered and it took all her effort not to slap him.

"Yes, we do," she said, her throat drier that it had ever been.

The moment the door closed behind them, Joseph grabbed her by the arm again and headed her toward the livery. "I've arranged a buggy to take us home."

"To the old Wilson ranch?" she asked, her voice scratchy and barely audible.

He laughed. "I don't live there," he said. "I'd never heard of it until you mentioned it. You dear wife, are more gullible than I ever imagined, but you suit my purpose. We'll gather your clothing, and we'll be gone from this dump of a town forever."

Pearl fought back tears. What had she gotten herself into? More importantly, what on earth had Joseph Canning, if that was even his real name, gotten her into?

Joseph stood over his new wife as she packed the few meagre possessions she owned. He had grown quite fond of Pearl in a morbid kind of way, but it couldn't be helped.

He needed a wife, and that was all there was about it. The moment he'd set eyes on her in the mercantile, he was drawn to her. Her beauty and her fiery red hair set her apart from all others. He might even come to love her one day.

They had more than an hour's ride ahead of them. He couldn't risk staying around this area. "Pull your hair up into your bonnet," he commanded. The last thing he needed was for people to recognize her and start asking questions. He hadn't thought that part through, had he? He admonished himself for his poor planning.

He packed her valise onto the back of the buggy and helped her up. "I have to call at the bank on our way through," he said as he grinned from ear to ear. "If you try to run away, I'll go back and kill the preacher and his wife."

"You wouldn't dare." Her face had paled, and he knew then she would comply.

"You want to test out that theory?" She shook her head as he knew she would. He took up the reins and they set out, stopping at the bank. "Do not move an inch. You know I'll do what I said."

She nodded and sat ramrod straight.

He entered the bank and glanced about. This was going to be easy. Almost too easy. There were only two tellers, and two customers. He pulled the gun from his pocket and waved it about. He didn't even bother to cover his face.

"You two, in the corner and sit down." The customers complied. "You," he said, waving the gun right under the first teller's nose, "Fill this sack." He watched as the teller did as he was told. "Now give it to him." The second teller didn't wait to be given instructions.

Joseph backed out of the bank, a bag of money in one hand, and a gun in the other. He turned to his wife who was beyond pale. He hoped she wouldn't faint – he didn't have time for that nonsense.

"Here, grab this." He threw the money bag up to her and she caught it. For a God-fearing woman like Pearl, he was certain this would be the last thing she'd want to be doing. But with his murderous threat hanging over her, she wouldn't dare not obey.

He was quickly on the buggy and took off. Tears streamed down her face and he watched as she looked back over the town she loved so much.

"Why?" It was the only words she'd uttered since they'd left the bank.

His response was simple. "Why not?"

They pulled up outside a tidy-looking ranch some hours later. She was totally exhausted and mentally distraught. Who was this man she adored one day, and despised the next?

He'd hidden his true identity so well. She'd been such a fool – Pearl now knew who she'd been forced to marry. Joseph Canning was the notorious bank robber and head of the Canning gang. She'd read about him in the newspapers, but had never seen a photograph of him.

She wished she had. Things would be so different right now. Or would they? If he'd set his sights on her, the outcome would probably be the same, even if she'd known who he was.

She sighed.

"Come on, down you come." He grabbed her by the waist and held her tight, lifting her to the ground. "You really are beautiful, Pearl. I couldn't have chosen better."

She scowled at him. "I hate you," she snapped, but he ignored her, leaning in and kissing her.

When he finally pulled back, he was grinning. "Get inside and freshen up while I unpack the buggy." He unlocked the door and began to unload the buggy, grabbing the proceeds of the robbery first.

As if he could read her mind, her turned to her. "We've got business tonight." He wiggled his eyebrows then sneered, and she knew what she was in for. "Don't think about fighting me. I don't care how I make you my wife in more than name."

She gasped. Under duress was not how Pearl pictured her wedding night.

"Joseph, please," Pearl begged. "We've been married three months now and you still won't let me go to town alone?"

He stood towering over her and sneering down at her. He didn't care about her, not really. He'd made it crystal clear she was only there to cover up his illegal activities. What sort of bank robber marries and settles in one place?

The worst part was she knew he was right.

He pulled her close and hugged Pearl tightly, then kissed her passionately. It could only mean one thing – it always did. He was about to claim his husbandly rights, and she had no way of stopping him.

Pearl shoved the covers back and climbed out of bed. Joseph had finally had his fill of her and left. The door slammed as he went, then she heard the sound of horse's hooves not long after. It meant only one thing – the gang had been here. He'd probably told them all the things he'd done to her.

Heat rose in her cheeks at the thought, and tears rolled down her cheeks. How had she let herself be taken in by such a despicable rogue?

She stared down at her torn gown on the floor. Her so-called husband didn't care what he did to her, or to her clothes. She despised the man and had done since she was forced to marry him at gunpoint. There was absolutely no doubt in her mind he would have killed Preacher and Mrs Jones, and she couldn't allow that to happen.

After cleaning herself up and splashing cold water on her face, Pearl tied her hair back into a braid. She had planned to bake today, and Joseph's actions had put her behind.

She pulled on her apron and stoked the wood stove, then pulled all the ingredients out of the cupboard. She'd always loved to bake but having to do it under duress didn't sit well with her.

Pearl had added the last of the pies to the oven and was making coffee when someone began pounding the door. It wasn't Joseph, he never knocked. Her heart thudded – they never had visitors out here. They were too far out of town, besides Joseph didn't broadcast their whereabouts.

She gingerly opened the door, allowing only her face to be seen.

"Mrs Canning? Mrs Joseph Canning?"

The silver star on her visitor's chest told her this man was the law. "Yes," she said quietly.

"I'm sorry to advise your husband is dead. He was killed during a bank robbery." The sheriff looked like he was trying to subdue a smile. The law had been after her husband for some time.

She stumbled backward and her eyes filled with tears. Before she could stop them, hot tears ran down her face.

The sheriff stepped forward. "Let me get you some water," he said, pushing his way through the door. "I can see how upset you are."

Her head shot up. "Upset?" She began to laugh hysterically. "For that mongrel? He forced me to marry him at gunpoint and has kept me prisoner ever since."

The sheriff stared at her momentarily, then smiled. "In that case, Ma'am," he said, tipping his hat back from his head, "I'm very pleased to have been of assistance."

Chapter Two

For the next few days, Pearl celebrated in the only way she knew how. She baked her heart out, then went to town to try and sell her creations to the Mercantile.

Sunday worship was the one compensation Joseph had allowed her, but she could never go alone. This was her first foray into Whitehead unaccompanied. She'd never driven a wagon before, but was always willing to learn.

First stop was *Hancock's Mercantile*. Pleased at this turn of events, Charlie Hancock promised to buy whatever she could supply. This was going to be her only means of supporting herself.

Then Pearl headed for the newspaper office. She'd not read a newspaper since Joseph had forced her to marry him. She wanted to know what was going on in the world.

She tucked the newspaper under her arm and strolled around town, taking in everything. The school, the bakery, the blacksmith's shop, and every other building she spotted.

Never before had Pearl been able to wander freely – since the day she'd unwillingly married Joseph Canning. She'd been over their meeting in her mind a million times. She always came to the same conclusion; there was absolutely nothing she could have done to stop his hold over her.

He was evil through and through, and that was all there was to it. If only things had been different. He'd seemed so loving in the beginning. Pearl shook herself. Her ordeal was now over, and she needed to move forward, get past the atrocities he'd bestowed on her.

She decided to visit the church before heading back to the only home she knew; Joseph's ranch with all its bad memories and horrors of the past few months. She wasn't certain she could cope with remaining there, but what choice did she have?

At the church she prayed for the soul of her outlaw husband and thanked the Lord for her newfound freedom. She sat with the tattered family bible in her hands for some minutes contemplating her ordeal.

What if she hadn't had to close the store that evening?

That question had gone through her head almost every waking moment since she'd been abducted. She knew deep down he'd been watching her. He had surely chosen her for a reason – most likely because she was living alone and had no one to miss her or look out for her.

She knew she was right and hugged the bible to her chest, then prayed. *Dear Lord, forgive me for hating him*, she prayed, then quickly left.

Pearl was loving it out here on the ranch. The Canning gang had made her life hell, demanding food and coffee. They'd demanded her body too, but Joseph had drawn a line with that. She was *his woman* and had no intentions of sharing her.

He'd even pulled a gun on a gang member early on, and she'd had no problems with any of them since. With the rest of the Canning gang languishing in jail, due to hang in the next few days, she need not worry about any of them turning up and claiming her as their own.

She went outside and let the chickens out, then collected up the eggs. She took the eggs inside and then fed the horses.

With the chores out of the way, Pearl made herself a coffee and sat at the well-worn table and began to read the newspaper. Staring up at her was her dead husband's face. News of his death was on the front page.

She quickly turned the page. There wasn't much she was interested in and she continued to flick through the thin newspaper. When she arrived at the advertisements, she decided to read them just for fun. She had no money to buy anything.

The words were big and bold, and Pearl couldn't help but notice them.

Mail Order Bride Wanted.

Thirty-something single man looking for bride. Has well-respected job, and needs pretty wife willing to cook and clean house.

Reply to Alex Farley c/o Grand Falls, Montana

Pearl continued to read the advertisements. There were three more calls for mail order brides, but for some reason, her eyes kept going back to the first one.

Perhaps the words *well-respected* were what drew her in? After what she'd been through, she needed a change of pace, she was certain of that.

Someone wanted to buy a horse, another wanted some chickens, and someone else was looking for two pigs so they could breed.

She couldn't help but snort at the latter, but her eyes were drawn back to the first advertisement she'd seen.

Could she become a mail order bride? Would she even want to?

Her head was spinning. Pearl knew she couldn't stay where she was for long. Even with her sales to the mercantile, money would run out sooner than later. She snatched up some paper and a pencil and began to write.

Dear Mr Farley, she wrote with a shaky hand. *I would be happy to marry you.*

Pearl stared at the hastily written words and knew it was all wrong. She tore up the note and began again.

Dear Mr Farley, I am a young widow and saw your advertisement for a mail order bride. I can cook and clean, and have been told I'm pretty. I'm not short, but neither am I tall, and my long hair is often called fiery.

I've been left with no money to spare.

She re-read her words and shook her head. That last line was sure to put him off. She didn't want to sound like a gold-digger.

She re-wrote her words on a fresh piece of paper, leaving that last line off and carefully signing her name then added c/o Whitehead Post Office.

As she stared down at her words, she wondered if she was doing the right thing. What if he guessed she was Joseph Canning's widow? She snatched up the newspaper again and read the article about her dead husband. She sighed with relief when her name was not mentioned.

It was then she discovered the newspaper was few weeks old.

Of course it was – the article was written just after the notorious Joseph Canning was killed. That made her wonder if Mr Farley was even still looking for a wife.

She would send her letter anyway. If he'd since married, he wouldn't reply, so no harm done. Pearl found an envelope and addressed it, then carefully folded the letter and popped it inside. She sealed it and decided to go into town tomorrow and post it.

~*~

Grand Falls, Montana

One month later

Alex Farley strolled to the post office. "Morning, Cecil," he said, tipping his hat to the mercantile owner.

He almost collided with Mrs Baker from the diner. "Morning Mrs Baker," he said politely. "I didn't see you there."

"Good morning, Sheriff," she said, smiling brightly. "I've just made a new batch of muffins if you'd like one."

"No time now," he said, wishing he did have the time. A muffin and coffee would really hit the spot, and Edna Baker made the best muffins in town. Heck, she made the best everything in town. "But thanks all the same." He tipped his hat and continued on his quest.

The door to the post office was closed, which meant Abner Ackerman was likely delivering a telegram or a package. He leaned against the locked door and pulled his hat down over his head. Resting his eyes was not something Alex Farley did a lot, but there were no criminals around here, and no illegal activity going on that he could see.

He should be safe to rest his eyes for just a bit.

"I hope you haven't been waiting long, Sheriff," Abner told him, pulling his keys out of his pocket.

"Not long," Alex responded as he followed the postmaster inside. "You wouldn't happen to have any mail for me, would you?"

It had been nearly two months since he'd placed the advertisement and he was beginning to worry he'd lucked out. Perhaps he should ask Mrs Baker to help him write the next one, but then again, he didn't want the whole town knowing his business. If there was a surefire way of getting word around, it was via that lady.

He couldn't help but chuckle. She was a nice old bird, but she sure did like to gossip.

Abner went behind the counter. "As a matter of fact, I think I do."

The Sheriff's heartbeat quickened. After all this time, had he finally found a bride? Not that he should even be considering marriage. With a job like his, he could be gone for days or even months at a time.

But the thought of a warm body in his bed, and hot food on the table every night was a big drawcard. While ever he was in town, he ate at the diner. Otherwise he lived on cold beans. Edna Baker was an amazing cook, and he could order something different every night for a week before he had to start over.

If he could find himself a wife to do the same, he'd be happy. He wouldn't mind a bunch of little Sheriff's running around either.

Widow Baker was a little old for him – by about thirty years – otherwise she'd suit him fine. He chuckled to himself again.

"I know it's here somewhere," Abner said, bringing him out of his foolish ramblings. He reached up on his toes and stared into one of the pigeonholes. "Ah, there it is," he said. "Somehow got shoved to the back."

Alex reached out to take it. "Thank you kindly," he said as he took the envelope with the decidedly female handwriting. He put it to his nose hoping for perfume, but there was none. "Darn it," he said as he began to rip the envelope open, then headed back to the Sheriff's office.

The aroma of fresh blueberry muffins enticed him inside the diner, and he was soon sipping coffee as he read the short correspondence he'd received. He took another bite of muffin.

He must have read that letter four times over, trying to decide what to do. Alex wasn't much interested in marrying a widow – that could lead to all sorts of problems. The least of them being spoiled beyond redemption. If that proved to be the case, she'd get a rude awakening coming to this tiny western town.

He placed the letter back in the envelope and made the decision to accept. Hers was the first and only response, so there was little choice. She sounded suitable for his purposes anyway.

Alex swallowed down the last of his coffee and snatched up the muffin. He would finish it on the way back his office.

"Thank you, Mrs Baker," he said, and slapped some notes down onto the table. The lady was good to him, and he always left her a generous tip despite her protests.

"When are you getting yourself a wife?" she asked as he left the diner. She asked the same question every time her went there. Alex grinned at her but didn't say a word.

If only she knew.

Pearl awoke with a start. Her stomach was churning, and she was about to lose her supper. She threw back the covers and ran outside.

She only just made it in time. What on earth had caused this? She thought back to last night, and what she'd eaten. She hadn't felt particularly well, so she'd only had scrambled eggs and toast. She'd topped it off with coffee.

As she continued to empty her stomach, she was convinced it had nothing to do with supper. As she straightened up, she stared down at her stomach. Pearl rubbed her hands over her rather swollen belly, then stared up at the sky.

"Please Lord," she prayed. "Don't let me be having his baby."

The moment the words were out, she wanted to take them back. If she was indeed pregnant, she would love this baby with all her heart, despite knowing who its father was.

Bile rose in her throat and she threw up again. She had been certain there was nothing left to expel, but it seemed she was wrong.

When she was finally able to return inside, a thought struck her. It had been at least two months since she'd posted her letter to Alex Farley. It was a week since she'd checked in at the post office, so she would go there again today.

Before she left though, Pearl decided to write to him and let Mr Farley know she was pregnant with her dead husband's child. Whether or not his letter was there, she would post hers.

After all, it was the right thing to do.

Dear Mr Farley, since my last writing I have discovered I am carrying my dead husband's child. I will understand if you do not wish to marry me after all. Regards, Pearl Canning.

She addressed the envelope and sealed it ready to post.

Pearl freshened up after her earlier ordeal and prepared to go into Whitehead. She had some baked goods to take to the mercantile, which meant she would be able to fill her pantry with the credit she would receive. Her supplies were getting worryingly low.

What she would do without the money from her baking sales, she didn't know.

At first, she had worried people in town would judge her on Joseph's actions. She'd had no backlash to date, and decided if it hadn't happened by now, it probably never would.

After offloading her produce, she headed for the post office. "Ah, Mrs Canning," Harry Smith greeted her. "I have a letter for you. It's marked important," he said with a wink.

"Thank you, Mr Smith," she said as calmly as she could. Her heart thudded – was she about to become a mail order bride? In all honestly, it couldn't be anywhere near as bad as she'd endured at the hands of Joseph Canning. "I would like to post this letter if you don't mind," she said handing over the letter and the correct postage."

She took her letter and stumbled outside. Had she done the wrong thing writing away to a total stranger? She would have to swallow her fear – Pearl needed a stable life and becoming a mail order bride was the only way she could achieve that.

She glanced down at her ever-growing baby bump. It was some months since she first wrote to Alex Farley, and she wasn't sure she wanted to open the letter. It could be a flat refusal.

She crossed the road and sat down on the wooden bench outside the bakery, then swallowed hard. This was it – the moment of truth.

She had stared at the envelope far too long already, and suddenly ripped it open, almost tearing the letter inside.

Dear Mrs Canning, the letter read. *You sound just like the sort of person I need as a wife. Unless I hear otherwise, I will transfer enough money for your travel and expenses.*

Kindest regards, Alex Farley.

Pearl was elated. Her fears had been expelled, and she would soon leave the place where her tortuous married life had begun.

But what of her soon-to-be husband? He hadn't revealed much of himself. What was his vocation? He'd mentioned being well-respected in his first letter, but what did that even mean?

She straightened her shoulders and made the decision to accept his proposal. After all, what choice did she have? She was widowed, pregnant, and with no money to her name. She would receive little for the sale of the horses when the time came, and the state had already seized the ranch. Allowing her to stay there a little longer was little compensation for the horrors she had endured at the hands of her husband.

Now she would wait. Mr Farley would send her enough money for the trip to Grand Falls, and within the week she would again be married.

Hopefully he would be a far better husband than Joseph.

Was she going from one bad marriage to another? Pearl shivered at the thought.

Her last task in town was to get checked over by the doctor. With everything that had happened recently, she needed to be extra careful of this baby.

She sat nervously waiting to be called. Finally the nurse ducked her head around the door and called her name. "Mrs Canning? You can come in now."

She was quickly introduced to Doctor Evans, who began his examination immediately.

The moment he'd finished he turned his back to her and began washing his hands. "How long did you say you've been married," he asked thoughtfully.

Pearl frowned. Why did that even matter? "It would be six months next week. Is there a problem, Doctor?"

He dried his hands and turned to face her again. "Not a problem, but you must have fallen pregnant close to your wedding night. This baby is at least five months, possibly closer to six."

"How could I have not known I was pregnant? That doesn't make sense." She would have, wouldn't she?

"You lost your husband recently. Hmmm? Stress can do a lot of things to people, even block things out. Perhaps you didn't want to know you were pregnant?" He stared at her for long moments. "Hmmm?"

He was right. She had surely blocked it out, but not for the reasons he thought. Her life was so much better and she'd been enjoying her life of freedom on the ranch. She hadn't thought about a lot else lately.

Besides she was a small woman, and her belly wasn't that swollen, so what he said made perfect sense.

"You'll have a little bundle of joy in about three months, give or take a few weeks. Hmmm?"

Three months? She sure hoped Alex Farley got that letter in time.

Abner Ackerman entered the office as though his life depended on it. "Sheriff," he said breathlessly. "You have an urgent telegram." He bent forward trying to recover his breath, and Alex quirked an eyebrow.

What could be so important the man had nearly caused himself injury to deliver it?

He snatched up the telegram and read it closely, then sighed. Of all the times to be summoned to help with a case. He had other things to attend to – very personal things – and leaving town was the last thing he wanted to do.

Perhaps he could deny the request? He could get Ackerman to reply with a firm no.

He shook his head. It wasn't an option. He was the only Sheriff for miles around and he had a responsibility. He was obligated to uphold the law and bring justice to those who broke it. Besides, this sounded like the work of Hector Grenville. He'd been trying to nab him for other murders for far too long.

Alex sighed.

This wasn't new. These sorts of assignments came out of the blue all the time. He just wished it hadn't been now. Not when he was about to marry. On reflection, sending for a mail order bride had been a stupid thing to do. His type of work didn't make for good marriages. He'd seen it ruin a decent relationship more than once.

How many of his law enforcement friends were still married? He could count them on one hand. Why on earth was he putting himself through this angst?

And what about his potential bride? She had an expectation after his last letter.

Well, it couldn't be helped, and the soon-to-be Mrs Alex Farley would have to wait another day or three. "Thank you, Abner," he said, sitting down at his desk. "I have to leave for an assignment, but I should be back in a few days. If any correspondence arrives for me, please hold onto it until I get back."

"Sure thing, Sheriff." He watched the man's retreating back.

Alex finished up his near-cold coffee and locked up. He needed to pack a few things and then he'd be on his way. As much as he didn't want to go, he had no choice. Besides, an entire family had been murdered and he had to bring the killers to justice. That's what he did.

He pulled on his hat and left his office, locking the door behind him. He smiled at the thought that hopefully in a few weeks, that warm body would become a reality.

Chapter Three

Sheriff Alex Farley was bone weary. What had first appeared to be a simple assignment to catch a killer turned into a marathon. He'd followed his elusive suspect from place to place, and finally, after what seemed forever, and was likely somewhere around three months, he was returning home.

Finally he had Hector Grenville right where he belonged – in jail and due to hang in a matter of days. He was filled with satisfaction.

His only regret being that once on the right trail, days had rolled into weeks until he'd lost count. Alex was too busy to think of much else, and when his mind did turn to his bride, he felt a twinge of guilt.

He'd left her hanging.

More than likely she'd married someone else by now. He told himself repeatedly that would be the case. If nothing else, it appeased his feelings of guilt.

He stopped at a small stream some miles from Grand Falls, letting his horse rest up. They were close enough to make it home today, but he wasn't prepared to overtask his horse.

If that meant camping out another night, so be it.

He leaned up against a tree on the edge of the water, and let Jasper have his fill. He wouldn't wander off, he never did, so Alex pulled his hat down over his eyes and rested, never meaning to snooze.

When he awoke it was mid-afternoon – could they make it home before daylight left them? He thought so. The sun would be on the verge of setting, but he longed for his own bed after all this time.

Jasper had found a shady spot under a stand of trees, and his head shot up as Alex stood. They'd been partners for some years now and could read each other like a well-written book.

He pulled an apple from his saddlebag and rewarded the horse for his good service. Soon they would leave. Only a few hours of riding at most, and Grand Falls would be in his sights.

As he rounded the corner to his hometown, warmth flooded him. Alex came to a halt and took it all in. He was finally back home after all this time. His body ached, and his heart was happy. Never in his life had he been so happy to be home.

When he arrived at his property, he headed straight to the barn. Jasper deserved a good brush down, fresh water, and a bag of oats, and that's exactly what he would get.

His horse always came first.

Jasper nickered into his shoulder as Alex removed the saddle and reached for the brush. "You're my best boy," Alex told him gently. "You are loyal to the end."

He felt dead on his feet, but Alex continued to groom his horse until he was done. There were no shortcuts here. He would polish the saddle tomorrow. Right now, he was bone weary and needed to sleep – for a day or two if he could manage it.

Heading up to his cottage, he noticed a light through the window. His heart pounded. Who would have the audacity to break into the Sheriff's house while he was away? The next question that entered his mind was why hadn't anyone noticed?

His deputy was supposed to be covering for him while Alex had been away. He felt a twinge of annoyance.

He peeked through the window to the kitchen but couldn't see anyone. He gripped the handle and threw the back door open, hoping to startle whoever was inside. He was met with silence.

"Hello?" There was no response. "Anyone here?"

He listened carefully, then began a search of the house. A valise sat next to his bed, and an ornate hairbrush sat on the side table. On opening the wardrobe, he saw several gowns.

He frowned. Then a thought struck him. *He had a squatter!*

But where was she? He continued to search – his cottage was small. There weren't many places to hide.

The second bedroom was empty, as was the sitting room. Now he was puzzled. Alex pulled off his hat and placed it on the peg at the front door.

Mrs Baker – if anyone knew what was going on, she would. As he reached for the front door, he heard it. The scream was muffled, but it was a scream for certain.

"Dang blast it," he muttered as he headed for the bathroom. "What the heck are they doing in there?"

The closer he got, the louder the screams. He reached for the handle, but hesitated. Should he go in?

Well, it's your house. What are you waiting for? But he still felt guilty.

"Hello?" he said quietly as he turned the handle.

"Don't come in," a female voice said urgently.

"Who...?" He wanted so badly to open the door but wasn't sure what he would find.

"On second thought..."

The scream was so loud this time he wasn't sure what to think.

"Miss?" He opened the door a smidge and could see the back of her head as she lay on the floor, a towel under her head. She had flaming red hair. That triggered a memory he was sure he should know.

"Arrrrrrrrrggggggggggghhhhh!" Then she began to pant. "Boy, am I..." Pant. "Glad to see you." Pant.

"Oh." He suddenly twigged; "*my long hair is often called fiery*". But why was she screaming?

"The baby is coming right now," she yelled. "Get help!" She resumed panting.

Baby? What baby?

He shook his head trying to clear the fog. Alex had no idea what was going on, but if there was a baby coming, he wanted no part in delivering it.

"Right. Baby." The information still hadn't really sunk in, but the massive bulge on her stomach seemed to prove a point. "I'll go get the doc. I'll be right back."

"No!! You can't leave – the baby is coming now!"

"Now, now?" His head was spinning. He couldn't deliver a baby. Could he? He'd delivered calves in his time, but never a real baby. A human baby. He was floundering.

"Cover the bed in towels," she said between pants. "I am not having this baby on your bathroom floor."

"I'll be back." He ran around like a chicken without a head for about twenty seconds, then did what he was told. He was a Sheriff. He'd done things worse than this without panic. At least that's what he told himself.

He returned to the bathroom and waited for further instructions.

"Don't just stand there like a dummy," she told him. "Help me into the bedroom. This. Baby. Is. Coming."

He helped her to stand, but she was wobbly on her feet, so he swooped her up into his arms. He carried her through to the bed he'd already prepared.

Alex laid her down carefully, then stood over her, staring at her. "It's Pearl, right?" Lord help him if that wasn't who she was. If that was the case, he had no idea.

"Yes, I'm Pearl. Now hurry up and wash your hands, then get back here. It's com…" With that she screamed and pushed.

He felt like screaming himself. He wanted to tell her not to push, he sure didn't want to deliver this baby.

"You have to wait," he told her, and she began to laugh hysterically. *Great, that was all he needed – a hysterical woman about to give birth to a baby he had no idea about.*

He rushed out of the room, washed his hands thoroughly and grabbed more clean towels before returning to the bedroom. Or as he was now calling it, the birthing room.

He slapped himself mentally. He didn't sign up for any of this when he sent for a mail order bride.

"Mr Farley!" she screamed. "Hurry!"

He ran faster than he'd ever ran before, then glanced down at her. "I think it's far too late to be calling me Mr Farley," he said glancing down at the business end of things. "Call me Alex."

She screamed again, and then did a huge push. "Oh my Lord," he said under his breath. He could see the head. "This kid's got red hair like yours," he said, now in a state of absolute panic.

Not that he let her see that. He had to stay calm for Pearl. If he panicked, it might send her into a spin, then they'd be in a right mess. He put his hands to his heart, trying to slow it, hoping to clear his head as well.

"Another push or two and I think this kid will be here."

She screamed and pushed hard, grabbing the sides of the bed. He pulled the towels closer. He did not want to drop this kid like he'd almost dropped that first calf all those years ago.

"Again." Now he was getting into it. He concentrated on what was going on this end. This kid was going to arrive whether he liked it or not.

He glanced up when he got no response from her. "Pearl?"

"I'm tired. Too tired," she said, her eyes fluttering closed.

"No, no, no, no!" he yelled. It looked as though she was on the verge of collapse. If that happened, he wouldn't know what to do. He checked, and the baby hadn't moved since that last push. Dare he risk moving away to try and coerce her?

He was so torn, but he had to check on the mother. "Pearl," he said, brushing her hair back off her face. "You need to stay awake and help me deliver your baby. I can't do it alone," he said, then leaned in and kissed her on the forehead. He had no idea why he even did that.

She nodded. As exhausted as she was, she agreed, then began to push. He ran back to the baby. "Head's out. One more huge push and you'll be done." At least he hoped that would be the case.

She didn't answer. He glanced up to see her eyes fluttering closed again. "Pearl. Pearl!" he shouted. "You can do this!"

She opened her eyes wide and pushed harder than she'd pushed before. He reached for one of the towels, and just as well – the slippery creature came whooshing out quicker than he'd ever imagined.

He stood staring down at the tiny human in his arms. He was never one for talking much, but now words failed him. He'd helped bring this baby into the world. In his house, and on his bed, no less.

For a tough Sheriff, he sure was feeling right soppy about now. His eyes even leaked a little, and that hadn't happened since he was a little kid.

"Is the baby alright," Pearl asked. "It's not crying."

She was right, it wasn't. And he'd been too busy getting all mushy to notice it wasn't breathing. He grabbed it by the legs and held it upside down, then slapped its behind. Not too hard, mind you. It was a baby after all.

He watched and listened. Nothing. He slapped the baby's behind again.

There was a knock at the door. "Come," he screamed, and the door flew open. "In the bedroom," he shouted.

He glanced up to see Deputy Jefferson Cauldry standing there staring. He was surely in shock, just like Alex. "Don't just stand there, get the doc!"

Cauldry was off like a shot.

Alex stared at the baby. He could see tiny movement on its chest. There was a glimmer of hope. He put the baby to his shoulder as he sat on the edge of the bed, and began to pat it on the back, silently praying at the same time.

Suddenly, out of nowhere, the baby began to cry. "Praise the Lord," he said, tears streaming down his face.

He pulled a towel up over the baby to keep it warm. It was about then the doc arrived. "Thank God you're here, Doc. The kid wasn't breathing."

He wiped the tears away from his face with the back of his hand, hoping no one would notice them. Doc took the baby and did what had to be done. "Get up there and wake up the mother. Keep her awake," he said.

"Pearl," he said, sitting next to her on the bed. "Pearl, it's a girl," he said. "She has fiery red hair, just like yours."

Her eyes fluttered open. "Is she…alive?"

He swallowed – hard. He was filled with emotion. "She's alive. The doc is here now, so everything will be alright."

She reached out a hand and grabbed his. "Thank you," she whispered. "I don't know what I would have done without you."

He savored the feel of her hand on his. Her touch, and the emotion in her voice.

It was about then the doc came over and handed him the tiny bundle, wrapped in a clean towel. "The mother is too weak to hold the child, so it's up to you," he said, then winked. Did he think Alex was the father?

Doc propped an extra pillow behind Pearl's head, then checked her over. "She's going to need some rest, but she should recover nicely."

Alex stared down at his new family. When he sent away for a mail order bride, he hadn't expected anything like this.

More than anything, he was relieved he had made the decision to come home today and not camp out another night. He didn't even want to think about the outcome if he had.

Chapter Four

Alex collapsed on the spare bed.

He was already beyond exhausted before he'd arrived home, and now there was no name for it. He kicked off his boots and lay his head on the pillow.

He didn't even bother to throw back the covers. Besides, he wasn't going to sleep, just rest his eyes for a minute. At least that's what he told himself.

He'd cut up one of his better towels into diapers, then emptied out a drawer and lay the baby there after padding it out.

That was the best he could do tonight. Tomorrow though, was another story entirely. If Cecil at the Mercantile had no cradles in stock, he would make one himself. Baby Pearl needed a proper place to sleep; a place of her own.

His eyes opened wide. He couldn't call her Baby Pearl, even if she did look like her mother. Tomorrow he'd push Pearl to name her. That was just one of the important tasks he had to do tomorrow. The other was talk to Pearl about their future.

He hadn't signed up for a mother/daughter duo, but to be fair, he had disappeared for far longer than he'd anticipated. Did she even bother to write and let him know? He certainly hoped so. Another task added for tomorrow's list – check the post office.

Not that he didn't trust her, because he did. At least he thought he did. On reflection, she must have trusted him, to come all the way out here without him even sending her the fare. Why hadn't he done that before he left?

Because he'd been called out urgently and hadn't expected to be gone more than a few days.

Anger flared in him. Why had he been so selfish and not let her know he'd had to leave? He could have at least sent a telegram and some money to tide her over. She put herself and her baby at risk traveling alone in that condition. He could have made arrangements for her.

If he was truthful with himself, would he have done that? Would he have accepted another man's baby, without ever having known the mother?

His heart thudded. Hindsight was a wonderful thing, and even with it in play, he couldn't say what he would have done. He was a decent man and liked to think he would have done the right thing.

Now he admonished himself for not getting home earlier. He had no idea how long Pearl had been in labor. If he hadn't arrived when he did, it could have ended in disaster for both mother and baby.

He swallowed hard. *It would have been his fault.*

The whole situation was his fault. If he'd known, arrangements would have been made for her to be looked after properly. As it was, that dear baby had nearly lost its life.

Alex felt suddenly overwhelmed. Perhaps he was still in shock about the whole situation? Yes, that had to be it – he didn't normally have such rambling and devasting thoughts. Usually his head hit the pillow and he was dead to the world.

His belly rumbled, and Alex realized he hadn't eaten since breakfast. He'd intended to be home in time for lunch, but his unplanned snooze by the stream had messed up his plans.

He dragged himself of the bed and headed to the kitchen, then did a double take. What about Pearl? Would she be hungry?

He headed into the master bedroom instead. It felt rather creepy standing there looking over her while she slept, but he wanted to ensure she was fine. He pulled the covers up around her shoulders, and she rolled over.

He couldn't even begin to imagine how she had felt having a complete stranger deliver her baby. Even if that stranger was her betrothed.

A shudder went through him.

Tomorrow they had decisions to make. Did she still want to marry him? Indeed did he still want to marry her?

He stared down into her face. Worry lines surrounded her eyes. She wasn't very old, mid-twenties at most he guessed, and already she had the weight of the world on her shoulders.

A tiny hiccup tore his attention away from Pearl. Warmth flooded him as he gazed at the tiny cherub in the bottom drawer of his cupboard. Did he really bring her into this world? Emotion threatened to overcome him.

No wonder he couldn't sleep. His life took on a whole new meaning the moment he'd held her in his arms.

Bringing her back to life had been terrifying, but he was so glad he persevered. He had never been so glad to see another human being as he had when the deputy walked through his door.

Alex rubbed his hands over his face. He wanted to be this child's father. Was Pearl going to let him? She could disappear as quickly as she arrived. He knew so little about her – she'd needed a safe place to stay to have her baby. Perhaps she would move on once she recovered.

His shoulders stiffened. He certainly hoped not.

Tomorrow was another day, and they could sit and talk about it. About everything.

Either way, Alex knew he was not the same man he was when he woke up this morning.

The high-pitched screaming woke Alex up with a start.

He jumped out of bed and ran toward it, forgetting where he was. Pearl was wiping the sleep out of her eyes and swung her legs over the side of the bed. She reached down to pick up the baby.

He stared at her bare legs, then forced himself to pull his eyes away. Leaning forward he covered her up with the bedding.

"I'll change her. You rest."

He lay a towel on the end of the bed and snatching up a clean makeshift diaper, began to change the precious child in front of him. "She's wet through," he said, pulling the baby's nightgown over her head. "Do you have any extras?"

Pearl nodded toward the valise next to the bed. "In there," she said quietly.

It was obvious she was still exhausted, but going by the persistent screaming, Pearl would have to stay awake long enough to feed her baby daughter.

"I'll watch her," she said, putting a gentle hand to the baby's midriff.

He opened the case and found a small pile of baby clothes. There weren't a lot there, but they could make do for now. Alex found a nightgown and put it on the baby. He lifted her against his chest, and she immediately stopped crying.

His heart did a little skip. Was this what it was like being a father? He shook himself mentally. He wasn't the baby's father. Would he like to be? He told himself he wasn't sure, but he had a very special connection with this baby – he'd brought her into the world.

As quickly as she stopped, she began to cry again.

"I'll have to feed her," Pearl said quietly. "She's obviously hungry."

Alex stood rigid after handing her over. "Ahem." Pearl glared at him. "A little privacy?"

He almost laughed out loud. After what he'd done just hours earlier, and she was worried about him watching her breastfeed. He managed to control his outward emotion. This time anyway.

"Would you like a cup of coffee? Something to eat?"

She glanced up and smiled at him. "A cup of tea would be nice, thank you."

He left her to do what she had to do and headed toward the kitchen. It was then he realized he was wandering around in only his drawers. Embarrassment flooded him.

Well, he guessed neither of them got the privacy they wished for. A smile escaped him.

He stoked the fire and filled the kettle. It would be awhile before it was ready, so he got dressed while he was waiting. His stomach began to rumble.

He carried the lantern through the house, taking it into Pearl's room. "Will this help?" he asked, trying to avert his eyes.

"It will, thank you," she said, taking the baby from her breast and placing her on her shoulder. The moment the baby burped, she was placed on the other breast.

Alex stood there mesmerized. He'd never seen anything so special in his life, and he'd seen a lot. "Your tea will be ready soon," he said shakily, backing out of the room.

He longed to hold the baby again and longed to hold her mother.

What was wrong with him, he admonished himself. He'd been deceived and possibly used. He rubbed at his eyes. He was beyond exhausted, and his mind was running away all over the place.

By the time he returned to the kitchen carrying another lamp, the kettle was almost boiled. He would kill for a coffee, but that would render him even less likely to sleep.

He poured two mugs of tea and took one into Pearl. "I forgot to ask how you have it."

"Black, no sugar. Can you put it on the cupboard? I can't risk holding it with the baby."

He placed it on the cupboard, then reached out for the baby. "I'll hold her for you." He wrapped her in the tiny blanket she'd slept under, then cradled her to his chest again. The feeling that came over him was inexplicable.

They had important decisions to make, he and Pearl, and they involved this sweet baby girl. He glanced across at Pearl. She sipped on her tea and stared at him over the top of the mug.

"What are you thinking," he asked quietly, trying not to disturb the baby who was drifting off to sleep.

She pulled the mug away from her beautiful lips. "I'm thinking I made a mess of everything. I dropped a bombshell on you, there's no denying it."

He stared down into the face of the angel he was holding. "I should have been here. I was meant to be gone a day or two, and no longer."

Her eyes opened wide. "Oh."

She could have said far more, but that one word encompassed it all. "It's far too late now, but I'm sorry," he said. "I should have been here for you."

Her eyes welled with tears, and she watched him gazing at her as she fought to stop them falling. "The government took my husband's house soon after he died," she said quietly. "I had nowhere else to go."

The statement had him curious, but she looked as though she was ready to collapse. "Finish your tea," he said gently. We can talk more tomorrow."

"I've had enough," she said, and placed the mug on the cupboard. Alex handed the baby back, but she was far too exhausted to hold her, so he lay Baby Pearl down to sleep.

"Can you promise me one thing," he asked quietly.

She stared at him.

"Name this baby. I can't keep calling her Baby Pearl."

"Baby Pearl? I've never heard you say that."

He grinned. "It's what I call her in my head."

She laughed out loud. "I will, I promise. Tomorrow," she said as she lay back on the pillows. He watched as her eyes drifted closed; she was soon fast asleep.

Pearl glanced up at the table to see Alex staring at her.

He'd cooked her a wonderful breakfast of bacon, sausages, and eggs with toast on the side. A mug of hot tea stood in waiting for her.

She was very grateful for the pillow he'd slipped on the chair before she'd entered the kitchen. Sure, she felt embarrassed, but how much worse could it be than having a total stranger deliver your baby?

"Thank you," she said quietly, then reached across the table for his hand. His head shot up as she startled him. "Shall we say grace, or am I presuming too much?"

He smiled. "It's perfectly fine," he said, giving her hand a squeeze.

"Dear Lord," she said quietly. "Thank you for this food before us. Special thanks for sending the Alex to me in time, and for helping him save baby Maude's life last night. Amen."

"Amen."

She tried to hide the emotion threatening to come to the surface, and quickly let go of his hand and grabbed up her mug of tea.

"Maude, eh?" he said with a grin. "I like it."

Why did her heartbeat hitch up whenever he smiled at her? "It was my grandmother's name. She would approve of the likes of you." She couldn't help but grin, but heat rose in his cheeks. Had she really embarrassed him?

She thought so.

"Eat up," he said, indicating her food. "Before young Maude starts demanding her breakfast." He winked at her and her heart skipped a beat.

"Later we'll sit down and have a talk – work out a few things. Like whether you're staying or not."

Her heart thudded. *Did he want them to leave? And so soon after she'd given birth?* She hadn't figured him to be a cruel man, he'd seemed so caring, so loving.

Pearl was crying inside, but she had no intention of letting him see her heart was breaking.

"Let me know when you're ready," she said firmly, and his head shot up. He frowned but said nothing and continued to eat.

He was a big man, far bigger than she'd realized the night before. But then again, she'd been rather preoccupied last night.

He would be every bit of six foot to her five foot six. His dirty blond hair made her wonder what color hair their own children would have. That is, if he even allowed her to stay.

She wouldn't blame him if he sent them away. He had never agreed to accepting another man's baby. Heck, he didn't even know she was pregnant, despite her writing to let him know.

What a mess. Pearl had been convinced she could start her life over with a new husband.

She pushed her dishes aside as she began to stand, and he jumped up and raced around to the other side of the table. "Let me help you back to bed," he said gently, and placed his hand below her elbow."

She glanced up at him and frowned. "I need to clean this mess up first," she said. She would manage, she would find a way.

She stumbled as she began to shuffle toward the sink and Alex swooped her up. "Back to bed with you," he said. "I'll get the doc to come and check you over again today."

"I, uh,"

"No arguments," he said firmly. "I am more than capable of cleaning up." He helped her remove her robe and placed her carefully back into bed. Maude was still sound asleep. "You rest up," he whispered. "I'll check in on you later."

She nodded her agreement and was asleep the moment her head hit the pillow.

~*~

Pearl sat opposite him in the sitting room. Maude had been fed and changed and was now sound asleep.

"I'm really sorry for forcing all this on you," she said quietly, her eyes averted. "I didn't know what else to do." She twisted her hands in her lap, guilt overwhelming her.

"When did you arrive?"

She thought he'd be beyond angry with her, but he didn't seem to be. She glanced up at him. He seemed a little tense, but not irritated or annoyed. "About two months ago. I waited for your next correspondence, but then it was too late. The house was seized, and I had nowhere to go."

She stared at him briefly. "Except here."

He nodded.

"When I arrived, I discovered you were away on assignment. I admit I was angry with you, but then found out it was an emergency."

"I felt terrible leaving you in the lurch, but I had no choice." He went to the window and stood there staring out. "I felt more than a little guilty leaving you hanging like that." He spun around to face her.

He stared down at a pile of letters in his hands. "I've been to the post office this morning – while you slept. You were right, you let me know you were with child. Several times. Each letter sounded more desperate than the last." He swallowed hard. "I'm sorry I ever doubted you."

Maude began to cry, and Pearl stood. "You stay," he said gently. "I'll bring her here." Pearl's eyes followed him as he left the room. Whatever happened in the next half few minutes would determine her future.

The crying stopped, and she envisioned Alex with Maude on his shoulder. He would make a wonderful father, that much was already apparent. Maude had taken to him very quickly, and so had Pearl.

He didn't have to deliver her baby. He could have left her stranded and gone for help, but knowing it was too late, he'd stayed.

She was so glad he did.

She swallowed the emotion that was threatening to overtake her. Far too much had happened in the last twenty-four hours, and she didn't know how to process it.

When he returned to the sitting room, she outstretched her arms for her baby. "She's happy for the moment. Let's not disturb her," he said quietly. He was right of course, but Pearl was feeling protective toward her little girl, as a mother should.

She nodded her acceptance, and he continued to rub the baby's back as he sat down again.

He glanced across at her. "The question is," he said, his voice low. "What do we do now?"

She licked her dry lips and tried to speak, but the words wouldn't come out.

Alex frowned at her. "Pearl?" he said softly, and she turned her head away. She hated that she'd done this to him. It was eating her up inside.

"I, I am not going to make you marry me," she said, a lump in her throat. "Maude is not your daughter, and it's not your responsibility to look after her. Or me."

She quickly stood and took the baby from him, leaving him to stare after her.

Chapter Five

What just happened? Alex was stunned and stayed where he was for a full three minutes. Did she no longer want to marry him? He shook his head.

The original plan was for them to marry. Did she think because she now had a baby, he didn't want her? That was so far from the truth it wasn't funny. Perhaps because of what they'd been through together, the three of them, he felt a connection.

He couldn't be certain, but right now, he felt something for those two. It wasn't pity; he knew that much. It was a really strong connection, like they all belonged together. He prayed Pearl was not going to leave him – he wasn't sure he could cope with that. Not after everything they'd been through together.

He felt hollow inside, almost like someone close to him had died and he couldn't process it. He had no plan other than to marry Pearl and become Maude's father. There was no real reason not to do either. Was there?

His decision made, Alex stood, then went to the window and stared out again. He loved this place. Everyone was willing to help everyone else.

Did Pearl think she would be treated like an outcast here? That was far from the truth, he was convinced of it. And now he would tell her so.

As he turned away, he saw movement out the corner of his eye. He wasn't sure whether to hide or leap with joy, but Mrs Baker was heading for his cottage.

He opened the door before she had the chance to even knock. "Good morning, Mrs Baker," he said, a note of desperation in his voice. Could she be the solution to his problem? Could this dear old biddy convince Pearl to marry him?

"Yes, yes, good morning, Sheriff," she said impatiently. "Where is the little angel? You know I adore babies."

He couldn't help but grin. "Take a seat, and I'll see if she's awake." He indicated the sitting room, then disappeared down the hallway.

He put his head around the door to find Pearl sitting on the edge of the bed, Maude in her arms. It was obvious she'd been crying – her eyes were red and puffy, and her nose was red too. Alex sat down beside her and put his arm around her shoulders.

"Don't cry," he said gently. "We'll work it out, I promise."

She glanced across at him. "I don't think we can."

Tears welled in her eyes again, and he brushed her tears away with his thumb. "You have a visitor," he said. "Mrs Baker has come to visit with you and Maude. I'll take her while you clean yourself up."

She managed a small smile, then headed toward the bathroom. He glanced down at Maude. Could she be his daughter? It already felt like she was.

She was a dear little thing, and he felt such a connection with her, it would break his heart if either of them left. The only thing pacifying him right now was they had nowhere else to go.

He wandered out to the sitting room where Mrs Baker was waiting patiently. "She's asleep," he said quietly, and Mrs Baker nodded. She reached out her hands, and he reluctantly handed the baby over. He knew she was in no danger with the older lady, but he felt suddenly protective of her.

"She's beautiful." If he didn't know better, he'd think tears were forming in her eyes. Mrs Baker was known for being a strong woman, but she also had a softness about her.

Maude hiccupped and Alex reached for her. He put her to his shoulder where she seemed most comfortable. Almost at the same time, Pearl entered the room. She looked far better now, but it was still apparent she'd been crying. Mrs Baker stared at her momentarily.

"Congratulations, my dear," Mrs Baker said. "I heard you had a hard time of it."

"How did you..." Pearl's words hung in the air.

She glanced across at Alex. "Word travels fast in a place like this," he said gently. He indicated for everyone to sit down.

"So when you are you two getting married?" Mrs Baker was never backward in coming forward. Usually it amused Alex, but not today.

"I don't know if we are," Pearl said.

Alex spoke at the same time. "Today, if the preacher can manage it."

The older woman glanced from one to the other. Pearl looked embarrassed.

"You need a father for your baby," Mrs Baker said matter-of-factly.

"She has a father, but he died," Pearl said defiantly, then swallowed hard.

He glanced at her and frowned. "She needs a father who is alive," he said firmly. "I can be her father. I brought her into this world, after all," he said. "And brought her back to life when she wasn't breathing."

He glanced between the two women. Mrs Baker sat open mouthed, and Pearl glared at him. "I didn't need reminding of that," she said gruffly.

She looked ready to burst into tears. "Sorry, that was insensitive," he said, wanting to take his words back.

"It was," she said quietly.

"Perhaps I should leave you two alone," Mrs Baker said, looking decidedly uncomfortable. "Whatever you decide, I'm sure Preacher Devon will accommodate you." She stood and glanced at the baby again, then left without another word.

"Pearl," Alex said quietly, not wanting to get her hackles up again. "Marry me and I'll provide for both you and Maude." She stared at him but didn't utter a single word. "I already have feelings for you both, and I want to look after you."

Maude grunted and he looked into her face. She was turning red. "What's wrong with the baby?" he asked, suddenly alarmed.

"She's filling her diaper," Pearl said.

"Oh. As I was saying…we can get married today, then you know you'll both be secure and well looked after."

"I don't know…"

"Good grief," he said, a foul smell suddenly permeating the air. Pearl grinned. "You go change her, and when you come back, give me your decision. Alright?"

She nodded. Not really a commitment, but more a promise to think about his proposition. Well, it was really a proposal, but he didn't think she saw it that way.

He handed the baby over, and they left the room. No one told him babies could cause such a repulsive odor.

It was done.

Preacher Devon had kindly come to the house to marry them. Pearl was in no position to go to the manse or the church in her condition. Mrs Baker had come along as a witness, and she'd brought Doc Spencer's wife along as another witness.

It was far too much for Pearl – she looked totally exhausted. He settled her down after everyone had left, then went out to the barn. Poor Jasper had been neglected. "Hello boy," Alex told him, then filled his feed trough. "Have I got a surprise for you." He chuckled to himself as he filled Jasper's water.

He reached for the horse's brush, and gave him a good grooming, satisfied his partner wasn't going to suffer over everything that had happened since they'd arrived home.

Now he felt comfortable going to the Mercantile.

He strolled along the boardwalk toward his destination and pondered the last twenty-four hours. This time yesterday he was snoozing on the edge of a creek without a care on his mind. How did he get here?

He shook himself mentally. He wasn't too upset with the turn of events, and now he needed to concentrate on buying supplies for Maude.

Both Cecil and his wife Hannah were in the Mercantile, which worked out well for Alex. He knew little of babies or their needs.

"Good afternoon, Sheriff," Cecil said. "What can I do for you today."

Alex could tell he wanted to say more but held back. No doubt he'd heard about Pearl and the baby. "Howdy Cecil, Hannah. I need some baby supplies, but not sure what I need."

He glanced into the main part of the store but couldn't see anything of interest.

"That's more Hannah's department," Cecil said with a grin, "So I'll leave you to her." He glanced down at their daughter who was happily playing in the enclosure Cecil had made in a corner of the store. She was contained but could see her parents, as well as play to her heart's content.

"What do you need, Sheriff?" Hannah was a fine-looking woman, polite, and always helpful. Being a mother herself was helpful.

He shrugged his shoulders. "Honestly, I don't know."

Hannah stared at him momentarily. "What do you have, if it's not too impolite to ask?"

Alex didn't have to think. "Some clothes, one blanket and a few diapers I made out of a towel as a matter of urgency after the baby was born last night." He sighed. "She's sleeping in a drawer right now." It sounded worse when he said the words out loud.

Hannah's eyes opened wide. "Oh my. Follow me." She took him to a corner of the store dedicated to infant supplies. "We don't carry a lot of items for babies because most people order ahead. We have a cradle – you'll need that for certain." She pointed to another part of the corner. "There are diapers and muslin wraps over there, and some gentle soaps you'll need to bath a baby."

Alex glanced around. Where should he start?

"Oh, and you'll need a bucket for the soiled diapers."

"I'll take the cradle for certain. Does it come with a mattress? Give me two dozen diapers, two muslin wraps and some of that soap. Anything else I should get?"

"Do you have soft towels? You can't use rough towels on babies."

"I tell you what Hannah – you put together whatever you think I need. Some more nightgowns and booties would be good too. She doesn't have much of anything."

"Leave it with me," Hannah said, not even blinking an eye. "Cecil will help you take the cradle home, then you can come back for the other items later."

A weight seemed to lift from his shoulders at her words. "I'd best take some of those diapers with me," he said. "We're almost out. I had no idea babies went through so many diapers." He shook his head. "Thank you, Hannah," he said genuinely. "I really do appreciate your help."

Cecil arrived and they carried the cradle out the door together. He didn't say a word until they'd left the store. "The child will change your life, you know," Cecil told him. "When Hannah arrived with a baby, I was ready to send her back."

"There was no sending this one back," Alex said, chuckling. "She was forcing her way into this world whether I wanted her to or not."

Cecil laughed along with him. "That so? Well, you won't regret it."

Alex nodded and they continued on it silence. It wasn't far to his house, so that was good. Not that the cradle was heavy, it was just awkward.

He would need to set it up in the spare room. He went over in his mind how he would move the current furniture around to fit it in.

He opened the door, and they maneuvered the cradle through the front door and down the hallway. There was no sign of Pearl, so he figured she was still asleep. It would be a nice surprise for her when she awoke.

"Do you have a minute to spare while I move this bed across?" Cecil agreed. "I apologize. I didn't think you would have one of these in stock."

"Let me help. Many hands make light work, as they say." He'd not had a lot of interaction with Cecil, but he'd always been friendly and helpful.

"I appreciate it." They moved the bed across, then set about moving the cradle into the room. "All done. Thank you."

Alex checked on Pearl, who was still sound asleep, and the two men went back to the Mercantile together. "Rosie is getting big," Alex said making conversation. It had been some months since Hannah and Rosie had arrived in Grand Falls.

"She really is. It won't be long, and we'll wonder where the years went." He stared at Alex. "Appreciate the time you have with Maude, because they grow up before we know it."

He was sure Cecil was right, but at this very moment, he wanted to ensure he had everything he needed to keep Maude safe and warm.

When they arrived back at the store, Hannah had a bundle of items waiting for him. "I've given you the basics here – towels, bibs, knitted booties and mittens, undershirts, diaper pins, something for diaper rash, and some muslin wraps. Oh, and some nightgowns."

He flicked through the items. "Is that everything I'll need?"

Hannah closed her eyes tight, trying to think. "Some soakers for the diapers would be good, and a tub to bath the baby. It depends on how much you want to spend."

"Whatever it takes. If you have those in stock, I'll take them now. If not, can you order them for me?"

"We have them," Hannah said. "Give me a moment." She went out to the storeroom and collected the tub. "I'll just grab the soakers, and you're done."

Cecil had almost finished adding all the items onto Alex's account by the time she returned. "Do you need a hand carrying those? I don't mind coming back with you," he said.

Alex lifted the tub, checking the weight. Everything had been placed inside it. "I'm sure I'll be fine, but thanks for the offer," he said.

Cecil finished up the account, and Alex was soon on his way. He was quickly discovering babies were expensive, but Maude was worth it.

He moved quietly into the house not wanting to disturb Pearl and Maude. He laid everything out on the spare bed, which for now would have to double as a makeshift table. The tub would have to go into the bathroom, but he would leave it here for now so Pearl could assess her supplies and decide if she needed anything else.

Right on cue, Maude began to wail. That in turn woke Pearl, who staggered out of the bedroom carrying the baby. "She's wet through and we're out of diapers."

"Not anymore," he said gently. "I picked up a few supplies at the Mercantile. If there's anything missing, let me know and I'll organize it."

He indicated for her to step into the spare room. He watched her surprised expression and felt relief. He was terrified she'd be upset at him shopping without her there. But the truth was, Pearl was not in a situation to go shopping right now.

She turned to face him. "Oh Alex," she said, looking close to tears. "This is wonderful. You are wonderful." She moved closer and hugged him, still holding the baby. Warmth shot through him.

He was caught off-guard by her next words. "Maude is not even your daughter," she said quietly."

He felt a small burst of annoyance, but he understood what she meant. "She is now," he said. "Just as you are my wife. We will be a happy family. Just give it time."

She nodded, and Alex felt relieved. His hope was they could be a happy family. Perhaps they would add to their brood as time went on. That was, if Pearl wanted that too.

As he lay a clean towel on the bed ready to change Maude, he wondered how long it would take for her to come around to his kind of thinking.

Chapter Six

Supper was a quiet affair. Maude was sleeping, and Pearl felt far more refreshed tonight than she had this morning.

Alex had let her sleep, and it had made a huge difference. She'd had no idea giving birth would take so much out of her.

Her new husband was a quiet sort of chap, but as she was learning, he was thoughtful, and very loving toward Maude.

"Mrs Baker made supper for us," Alex told her, indicating the beef stew in the center of the table.

"That was very kind of her," Pearl said, reaching for a warm bread roll.

He reached across and covered her hand with his own. "She's a kind person," he said.

She glanced down at his hand covering hers and pulled her hand away from the zing that went through it. "Just because we're married," she began. "Doesn't mean we should act like a married couple." Pearl still wasn't sure how she felt about marrying him, especially since it was only to give Pearl and her daughter stability and respectability.

The more she thought about it, the more she realized being a widow meant she would not have been taunted over her daughter's birth. But it was too late now.

Pearl always thought she would marry for love. So far, her life was a total wreck and she had no idea who she could trust. Including her new husband.

"I know the last couple of days have been very overwhelming, but for Maude's sake, we need to be like a real family." He sounded hurt, and if she was honest, his words shocked her. At this point in time, Pearl wasn't sure what she wanted. She'd married him because everyone told her it was the best thing to do for the baby. But what about her?

To be fair, she'd already promised Alex to marry him, but that was before either of them knew there was a baby involved. She didn't want to force him into a situation where he felt he had to support them.

It was already too late for that. They were married, so she had to live with that. At least for now.

Her plans for the future were sketchy at most. Once she'd recovered completely, she could leave and take Maude with her. She would get a job and support her daughter herself, instead of relying on a man who only married her out of pity.

At least that's what she'd thought. Then he went and bought half the Mercantile to look after his new daughter.

"This is delicious," she said pulling herself out of her wayward thoughts and taking a mouthful of the stew. "Mrs Baker is a great cook."

He grinned at her. "It's why the diner is so popular." He filled his mouth again.

Reaching for another bread roll, Alex glanced across at her. "We need to talk about the sleeping arrangements," he said, a worried expression on his face. "I know it's early days, but the situation has changed. We'll have to share a bed from now on." He said the last words quickly, as though perhaps he thought she wouldn't notice or understand them if he rushed.

She shook her head. "They don't need to change." She wasn't ready to sleep with him – a stranger – even if he was her legal husband. She'd already been forced by one man, was this marriage going to be no different?

"I, I can't sleep in the spare room now that Maude is in there," he said firmly. "I promise not to touch you." He glanced up and studied her. "You have just given birth after all."

She swallowed hard. The more she knew him, the more she liked Alex. She thought this would be so easy. Have the baby, then leave. But he had been nothing but caring and thoughtful. Plus he had a real affinity with Maude. If you didn't know, you would have no idea he wasn't her natural father.

Emotion threatened to overtake her. Perhaps she would stay for a week or two and then make her decision.

Yes, that's what she would do. Pearl finished eating, then sipped her coffee. Alex finished up and dished up Apple Pie, also made by Mrs Baker. Tonight, they were spoiled. Starting tomorrow, she would start acting like a wife.

Her decision made, Pearl picked up her spoon and began to eat the equally delicious pie.

The night was chilly despite it being Spring. Alex had lit a fire in the sitting room, as well as their bedroom.

Their bedroom.

It sounded strange for Pearl to be thinking that way, but the two were to share a bed starting tonight.

Alex had been a total gentleman. He sat in the sitting room reading his bible, allowing her to change into her nightgown in complete privacy. She was pleased that he had. The whole situation was awkward and undressing in front of him would have been even more difficult.

She hadn't said a lot, but she'd been grateful and overwhelmed at Alex's generosity. He didn't have to go out and spend so much money on her daughter.

She mentally corrected herself – *their daughter.* Now they were married, Maude was also his daughter, and watching them together, you wouldn't know he was not her natural father.

He stared at Maude with nothing but love in his heart. Perhaps he was after all the decent man she'd always dreamed of marrying? She certainly hoped so.

After undressing and donning her nightgown, she began to fold her clothes and placed them on a chair. She hadn't thought to ask Alex where she should put her clothing. It seemed strange to be standing in his bedroom waiting to climb into bed. This, despite having slept there the past couple of nights.

The change of dynamic, the two of them sleeping there instead of just her, had put a whole new perspective on things.

She threw the covers back and scurried across the bed. It was then she heard the bedroom door open. She pulled the covers up to her face, with only her eyes showing.

What she'd endured in Joseph's bed was beyond comprehension. Not once had she agreed to his so-called lovemaking. Forcing himself on her night after night did not make for a happy marriage.

She stiffened as he got closer to the bed and was shaking. Would he be true to his word? She certainly hoped so.

"Everything alright?" he asked quietly, glancing across at her.

She nodded. "Yes." It wasn't true and she knew it but had no intention of telling him so.

Alex pulled his shirt up over his head, and for the first time she saw the extent of his muscles. He was certainly a good-looking man, dressed or undressed.

He pulled off his belt, and then his breeches, laying them on the chair on top of her clothes. "We'll sort out the cupboard space tomorrow," he said. "I know you have some gowns in the wardrobe, but you'll need space for your, er, delicates too."

Heat rose in his cheeks. It took all her effort not to laugh.

"I'm getting in now," he said, standing there in his drawers. Pearl couldn't help but stare. Any other time, and any other situation...

No, she couldn't think like that.

He turned off the lantern, and without warning, he was in the bed and lying next to her. "Goodnight, Pearl," he said quietly.

"Goodnight." She rolled over to face the wardrobe, and he rolled over too. His cool skin hit hers, and they were lying closer than she was comfortable with, his hard body up against hers.

"I'm glad you came, despite my silence," he said gently. His hand slid around her waist and settled on her still swollen stomach. She stiffened.

"How are you feeling tonight? You had a real time of it."

She wriggled about, hoping he would move away. He didn't. "I'm tired, but apart from that I'm fine."

"That's good to know. The doc is happy, so that makes me feel better. He wants you to rest up though." His voice was a little stern this time, and although it rankled a little, she appreciated his concern.

He pulled her even closer, and this time she didn't mind. It felt nice to have someone concerned about her, to not hold her for only one reason.

As much as she tried to block the memories of her former marriage, it was hard. Really hard.

As if on cue, the baby began to wail. "I have to feed Maude," she said, trying to climb over him. She felt his breath against her cheek as she did so, and sensed his lips were ever so close. Pearl's breath hitched in her throat.

She fought against her need to kiss him, and felt his hands go up around her waist. "You stay," he said gently. "I'll change her and bring her in here for you to feed. It's warmer in here."

He lay her back down, and she felt nothing but gratitude for this caring and considerate man she'd married. She was beginning to think she'd done the right thing marrying him after all.

Chapter Seven

Pearl awoke wrapped in Alex's arms. She'd slept better last night than she could remember sleeping since the day she was kidnapped.

Having no idea of her future may have been the reason. With her valise on the floor on one side of her, and Alex on the other, she was stuck. At least she felt as though she was. She decided to climb across him, but could she do it without waking him?

She half sat and analyzed the situation. It would be tricky, and she was sure it would hurt a little, but she would try. As her leg stretched across his belly, pain filtered through her. Of all the stupid ideas she'd had, this would have to be the worst.

She tried not to cry out, endeavoring not to wake Alex, but the pain was so intense, she couldn't hold it back.

His eyes flew open and he suddenly frowned. "What on earth are you doing?" He looked thoroughly annoyed. Tears trickled down her face at the agony she was enduring. He grabbed her by the waist and lay her back down.

"I, I was going to check on Maude," she said quietly. "Then prepare breakfast."

He looked even more annoyed. "You're supposed to be resting. I'm not working at the moment, so it's no hardship for me to do those tasks." He sat on the side of the bed, his back to her, then pulled on his breeches.

As he stood, he pulled the covers back up to keep her warm.

He leaned forward and gently kissed her lips. "You look so cute with your hair all disheveled and that just awake look on your face."

She stared at him in disbelief.

"I could get very used to it," he said, then left the room.

When she thought about it, she knew he'd meant it in the best possible way. But she was so used to being abused and wasn't used to compliments. It was time to change her outlook on life.

She could hear Alex talking to Maude in the next room. He'd become very proficient at changing her diaper, and dressing her, and had even helped bath her yesterday. He was an absolute natural and she wondered why he hadn't married before.

The answer was obvious – his job kept him away from home far too much. She swallowed. Was that going to be the case with her? Was she going to get so enamored with the man she would miss him when he was away?

She didn't intend to stay around long enough to find out.

That thought caused her heart to skip a beat. She was getting far too comfortable with Alex Farley for her own good.

Pearl glanced up as he entered the room with her baby. She lay gently over his shoulder, covered in a wrap for warmth, and his expression was one of love. When he held her, Maude rarely cried – it was as though she knew he had saved her life.

A lump formed in her throat. She owed so much to this gentle giant. More than anyone would ever know.

He glanced up and stared at her. He looked at her the same way he looked at Maude, and she liked the feeling she got when he did.

She admonished herself. She was becoming far too soft and put it down to hormones. Having a baby messed up your whole body. Thankfully things would go back to normal in the months ahead.

Alex handed baby Maude to her. "She was far drier this morning, thanks to the soaker, I'm sure." He smiled at her, and her heart fluttered.

Her bottom lip suddenly quivered, and she felt like crying. How could she have been so lucky as to land herself this man as a husband? After what she'd been through, it seemed impossible.

He sat next to her on the bed, still holding the baby. He gently caressed her cheek, while keeping the other hand on Maude. "Tell me what's wrong," he said softly.

Tears flooded her cheeks, and she wasn't sure how to answer. "Why are you so nice to me?"

He frowned. "You're my wife, for one, and the mother of my daughter." She held out her hands and he handed the baby over to be fed. "Besides, I really like you."

He wiped her tears away and handed her a kerchief. "I'll leave so you have privacy," he said gently, then left the room.

She really had won the jackpot with him.

Maude was fed and sound asleep again.

Pearl dressed and headed to the kitchen to make breakfast, but apparently Alex had beaten her to it. The aroma of bacon and eggs drifted down the hallway. The closer she got, the stronger the smell.

He spun around as she entered the kitchen. "Good," he said. "You're right on time. Coffee's on the table, and I was about to dish up." He turned back to the stove and she stepped toward him, then slipped her arms around his waist.

"Thank you," she said quietly. "For everything."

He spun in her arms and was suddenly facing her. He stared down into her face, his eyes gazing at her lips. "You don't have to thank me," he said quietly, a quiver in his voice. He leaned down and claimed her lips.

His kiss was ever so gentle. Right now, she wasn't sure how she felt toward him, but his kindness overwhelmed her. If she was truthful with herself, she wanted to kiss him too, and that's exactly what she did.

They stood entwined for some time, her head resting against his chest, until he pulled back. "Darn it," he said. "The food is burning." He snatched up the frying pan and dumped it in the sink.

She laughed and he joined her. "I'm taking over the cooking. You sit and have your coffee."

He frowned but did what he was told.

Was this the start of some sort of relationship? She certainly hoped so.

~*~

Four weeks had passed since Pearl had given birth and they were all settling into a routine.

Alex had gone back to work, but not until he was certain she could cope on her own. Maude was such a good baby and was never any trouble.

Pearl felt she was recovering well, and her check up with Doc Spencer today had proven that. She knew Alex would be pleased too.

He was like a mother hen clucking over her chicks. The thought brought a smile to her face. She stood at the center counter making biscuits. She had always loved to cook and was glad to be back in a kitchen.

Her kitchen.

She glanced about. This place felt like home. She didn't know why except perhaps there was love here. That thought made her pause.

Did she love Alex? To be honest she hadn't thought about it before. But all thought of leaving him and taking Maude had left her over the past couple of weeks. She'd grown very fond of him and missed him when he was working.

Thankfully, his work had not taken him away since Maude was born. She added the biscuits to the floured tray and put them aside, ready to go in the oven when Alex got home.

It had been in the back of her mind to tell him about her ordeal with her first husband, Joseph. She didn't want him to find out in other ways. Being a Sheriff, he had the resources and the means to find out anything he wanted to know about her.

She glanced up as she heard the front door open. Alex was home. If he stuck to his usual routine he would stop in the nursery and check on Maude, then join her in the kitchen.

He came up behind her and wrapped his arms around her, then pushing her hair aside, kissed her neck. Her heart zinged.

She turned around in his arms and stared up into his face. "There's something I have to tell you," she said, feeling guilty for not telling him sooner.

"I know." He leaned in and kissed her, and she pushed him away.

"You know? What do you know?" She glared at him and shoved him aside so she could stir the hearty soup that was cooking on the stove.

Her heart beat rapidly. She wasn't sure if it was because he might know everything about her, or because she had to tell him.

"I know what happened to you," he said softly. "Why didn't you tell me?" He didn't sound accusing, rather curious.

She shook her head gently, then began to back away. He reached out and pulled her close. "You don't have to feel ashamed or guilty," he whispered in her ear. "None of it was your fault."

"I was a fool to trust him," she said against his chest. "I'm glad he's dead." She spat the last words, feeling relieved she'd finally said them. She glanced up at him. "Is that so terrible?"

He lifted her chin with his fingers. "Not terrible at all."

She relaxed against him again.

Her next words were difficult, and she kept her eyes averted. "Maude was not made of love," she told him quietly, her voice quivering.

She wondered if he'd guessed, because he didn't appear surprised. Alex lifted her chin with his fingers and stared down into her face. "That must have been horrible," he said. "I want you to know she is loved very much – by both of us." He tightened his grip on her as though he needed to do so to protect her, and they stood there for a very long time.

Finally his next words broke the silence. "I know we haven't known each other long, but I want you to know I have feelings for you. Strong feelings." His fingers caressed her cheek, and his arm around her was comforting. "In fact, I've fallen in love with you."

She glanced up at him. "I feel the same way." She got up on her toes and kissed him softly. "Perhaps tonight we can make it a real marriage?"

"I'd like that."

Pearl would too. All thoughts of running away had long left her. Alex was her forever man, that had become blatantly obvious almost from the beginning.

His head shot up suddenly. "That's Papa's girl," he said, as Maude began to wail. He gave Pearl a quick hug and headed toward the nursery.

Pearl watched his retreating back. What had she ever done to deserve such a wonderful man?

Epilogue

Two years later...

Alex paced the road outside their little cottage.

Pearl had been in labor for some hours now. His thoughts went back to the day he'd met her. At least this time she wasn't lying on his cold bathroom floor for hours without assistance.

Doc Spencer was with her this time, and they'd called in Doc Pendleberry from the Apothecary for back-up. After her last birth, they simply couldn't take the chance. Alex wasn't prepared to risk the life of mother or baby.

Standing outside the front door, he heard the unrelenting screams. He couldn't bear it and moved further toward town. This was to be their last baby. At least that what he thought. He couldn't stand the screaming, and the uncertainty.

He couldn't allow Pearl to go through this with each pregnancy. It broke his heart just listening to her now.

Maude was at the diner with Mrs Baker, so he headed down there. It would be hours before the baby would arrive, and they wouldn't let him inside, so there was no point him hanging around.

He was halfway there when he turned back toward home. *What was happening? Was Pearl alright? And what about the baby?*

The thoughts flooded his mind and he tried to chase them away, but they kept coming back. *What if he lost them?*

His heart pounded and a lump formed in his throat.

"Sheriff."

He turned around on hearing Mrs. Baker.

"Papa!"

Maude ran to him on her chubby little legs. She was such a blessing, and he treasured every moment they spent together. "Give Papa a kiss," he said gently, pointing to his cheek. She complied.

"Where's Mama? I miss her." She pouted and Alex pulled her into a hug, standing as he did so.

"Mama is having a little brother or sister for you. We'll see her later."

"Come back to the diner and have some coffee," Mrs Baker suggested.

He considered it but wasn't sure about the offer. "I might not have time."

"Believe me you'll have time. You want Papa to come to the diner with us, don't you Maude."

Her little hands cupped his faced. "Please Papa?"

How could he resist a request like that? "Alright, but I can't stay for long."

She clapped her little hands with glee, and his heart soared. His life had changed for the better the day Pearl and Maude had come into his life.

How he ever survived without them, he'll never know.

The moment they entered the diner, Mrs Baker pointed to a table. "Sit," she said firmly, and he did as he was told. No one would dare defy Mrs Baker.

She pushed a mug of coffee in front of him and he took a sip. "Thank you," he said. "I really need this."

He leaned back in the chair and tried to relax but it was impossible. He was far too worried about Pearl.

A feeling of dread came over him, and he tried to push it away, but it wouldn't budge. "I have to go back," he said as he stood. "Something terrible has happened, I just know it."

Mrs Baker stepped toward him and pulled him into a hug. "You would have heard if something bad had happened. But if it makes you feel better, go home and check for yourself."

"Thank you," he said quietly. "I need to do that."

Maude came running over as he headed toward the door. "Don't go Papa. I miss you."

Sadness overcame him. "I have to go, Little One, but you'll see me again soon." She hugged him and Mrs Baker held Maude by the hand as he left.

His legs felt leaden as he walked through the town. What he would find was anyone's guess. He stopped a few feet from his home, unable to keep going. His heart felt torn in two.

He stood in the middle of the road for what seemed a lifetime, but in reality, was about twenty minutes. The screams had subsided, and he was too afraid to go inside.

Finally the front door opened and Jesse Pendleberry called him in. "Congratulations," he said, a grin on his face. "You have a healthy baby boy."

Alex wanted to be happy, he really did, but what of Pearl. "Is Pearl..." He couldn't finish the question.

"Pearl is fine. Exhausted but fine."

For only the second time in his adult life, his eyes leaked. "Can I see them?"

Jesse slapped him on the back. "Of course you can." He held the door open for Alex, who almost ran through the door to his wife.

He moved quietly toward the bed. Pearl looked beyond exhausted, but after knowing what she'd endured last time, he wasn't surprised. At least this time she had professional help, so they were on the scene if anything went wrong.

Thank goodness nothing did.

"Alex." Pearl's voice was quiet, but she seemed pleased. "You have a son," she said, tears forming in her eyes.

He leaned in and gently pulled her into a hug. "Thank you," he said, and lay her back down again. He looked about. "Where is he?"

Doc Spencer stepped forward. "He's in the other room. We wanted to give him a thorough check after what happened with your daughter."

Jesse came in carrying the baby soon afterwards. "He's perfect. Not a thing wrong with him," he said, and handed him to Alex.

He looked down into his son's face. Emotion filled him, and he felt a deep love for this child. It wasn't unlike how he felt when Maude was born. At least this time he didn't have the angst of worrying if the baby would survive.

He walked over to Pearl. "Do you want to hold our son, or are you too tired?"

Her eyes were drifting closed. "Just a tiny hug, then I need to sleep."

Alarm bells rang with Alex. "Doc! Doc! Is Pearl okay? She can't stay awake."

Both men glanced up at him, then rushed over. "For goodness sakes, Alex. I'm just exhausted. You try pushing out something the size of a sack of potatoes and see how you feel."

He felt the heat creeping up his face. Pearl went to sleep, and he placed the baby in the same crib they used for Maude when she was born. At least this time their baby didn't have to sleep in a converted drawer.

The doctors packed up and quietly began to leave. "I can't thank either of you enough," Alex said, holding the door open for them.

"Glad to be of assistance," Jesse said. "Better safe than sorry, and after last time it wasn't worth the risk of not having help on hand."

He closed the door behind him and felt like he was ready to collapse. In the bedroom, Alex stared down at his exhausted wife.

"Lay down next to me, Alex," she said quietly. He did as he was told, and she was soon sound asleep.

"Papa! Papa!" Maude's words rang throughout the house.

Alex ducked his head around the bedroom door and opened his arms to his daughter. "There you are!" They shared a tight hug, then he carried her into the master bedroom.

Her little eyes opened wide at the sight of her mother and baby brother. "Baby!" She tried to wriggle out of his arms.

"Maude," he said firmly. "You need to listen to Papa."

She glanced at him but her little eyes kept wandering back toward the new baby. "Yes, Papa," she said quietly and looking a tad guilty.

Maude stretched her arms toward her mother who was holding the newborn. "You have to be gentle," he told her firmly.

She nodded her little head. "Yes, Papa."

"What are you going to do?"

She stared into his eyes. "Be gentle." Then she suddenly tried to jump out of his arms.

"Maude." This time he put on his stern voice. "Mama has a sore tummy, and baby will break easily. You must be gentle." He looked across at Pearl, who was totally exhausted. "This is not going to work," he said softly. "She'll have to wait until you are feeling better."

Tears rolled down the toddler's cheeks. "No, Papa! I be gentle."

He pulled her close and patted her back. "Show me how you can be gentle," he said, winking to Mrs Baker who had brought Maude back home a few hours after the birth.

Her little arms reached over his shoulder and patted him gently on the back.

Mrs Baker grinned. "She is such a sweetheart," she said. "Maude was a very good girl for Aunt Edna," she said.

"I maked muffins," Maude said excitedly. Alex glanced at Mrs Baker who rolled her eyes. Making anything with the over excitable child was not fun, but Maude enjoyed it.

One day she might be as good a cook as her mother.

His daughter hugged him tight then pulled back to look into his face. "Now Papa? I see Mama and baby now?"

What could he say to her sweet words? "Gentle, remember?"

She nodded her little head, and he placed her gently on the bed, sitting on the side of it himself. He took baby Jonah, and Pearl pulled Maude into a hug. "This is Jonah, your new baby brother," she said, indicating the newborn in his father's arms.

The toddler leaned forward and kissed the baby gently on the forehead. "Baby," she said.

"Baby Jonah," Alex corrected. "He has the same colour hair as you and Mama."

Maude glanced up to check. "My baby," she said, and leaned in again and hugged the baby ever so gently.

Alex couldn't be prouder. Despite their rocky start, they were a loving and happy family, and nothing would ever change that.

He couldn't imagine his life now without his wonderful wife and children, and thanked God for bringing them into his life.

No matter what happened, they would always be together.

The End

From the Author

Thank you so much for reading my book – I hope you enjoyed it.

Cheryl's other books in this series are:

Mail Order Millie
Mail Order Hannah

About the Author

Multi-published, award-winning and bestselling author Cheryl Wright, former secretary, debt collector, account manager, writing coach, and shopping tour hostess, loves reading.

She writes both historical and contemporary western romance, as well as romantic suspense.

She lives in Melbourne, Australia, and is married with two adult children and has six grandchildren. When she's not writing, she can be found in her craft room making greeting cards.

Links

Website: *http://www.cheryl-wright.com/*

Blog: *http://romance-authors.com/*

Facebook Reader Group:
*https://www.facebook.com/groups/cherylwrighta
uthor/*

Join My Newsletter:

https://cheryl-wright.com/newsletter/

www.ingramcontent.com/pod-product-compliance
Lightning Source LLC
Chambersburg PA
CBHW070632120726
47909CB00004B/1399